What Is ART?

Theater

Let's go to the theater

Today we went with Ann to the theater. It was awesome to see the stage, the curtains, the lights, and so many seats in the room! The play was very funny and full of animals—well, not real animals, but people who played the part of animals—and there were puppets that played the part of people. Everything is possible in the theater!

Curtain up

Once the play was over, we went with Ann and her friends to say hello to the actors. It was so exciting! Backstage there were many more people than onstage: The person in charge of the lights, the person in charge of the sound, the one in charge of the sets and props, the director of the play, and several musicians. And there were ropes, pulleys, trunks, props, and many other things everywhere!

Let's make faces

One of the actors, who was a bear in the play, told us that to act in a play you need to do only one thing: To represent just about anything.

For example, what face do you make when you are sad? And when you smell something nasty?

Paul makes an angry face; he covers his face with his hands, and when he takes them away, he looks very happy! Come on, let's make faces.

An imaginative body

"Now we will make it a little harder," the actor tells us. "We are going to imagine with our whole body. We are going to be ... robots!" And we all start acting like robots. Some walk and move their arms very quickly, while others move so slowly it seems their batteries have run down.

Our body allows us to adopt many postures, so we can become animals, puppets, acrobats, tables, hangers, trees, whatever. Do you want to try?

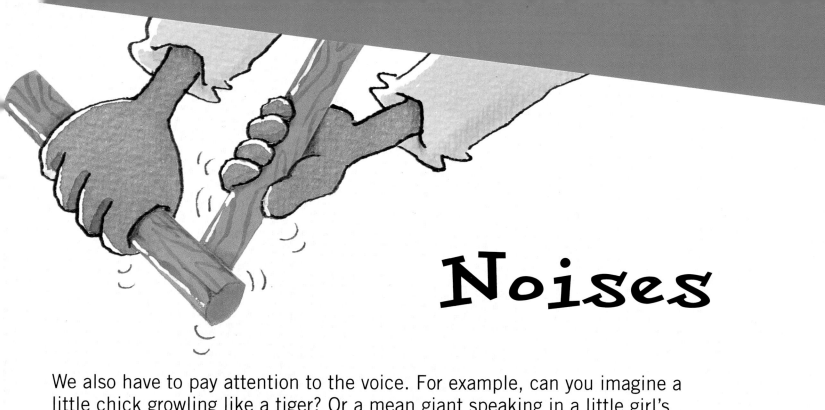

Noises

We also have to pay attention to the voice. For example, can you imagine a little chick growling like a tiger? Or a mean giant speaking in a little girl's voice? Let's try different ways of speech: Soft, fast, low, loud, or fast and slow at once.

And we can make noises using two sticks, a piece of paper, rice inside a jar, our hands, our feet … or our nose!

People and characters

Now we are going to act. Ann wants to be Little Red Riding Hood and Paul wants to be the wolf, but a good wolf. Ralph insists he wants to be a storm cloud, but ... how can you be a cloud? And after the rain, do clouds look the same or do they change their shape? And is Red Riding Hood tall or short? Happy or sad?

You can also make up characters—there are millions of possibilities!

The actor took us to a corner of the theater where there were trunks full of fabrics, ribbons, and hats. There were also big boxes, stickers, and a stapler. We had a great time making costumes and trying them on.

If we do not have fabric, we can use old clothes we find at home. With some imagination, socks can become gloves, a sweater can become a skirt, and so on. Give it a try!

14

A trunk full of surprises

Makeup anyone?

Later we went to the dressing rooms, where actors change into costumes and get ready to act out the play. What a mess! The place was full of makeup—pencils in all colors, jars with paint, and face powder. There were even false nails and eyelashes. We just loved makeup!

For our birthdays we will ask for face paint, so we will be able to make up our faces at home.

Once upon a time...

We have all thought about the character we want to play, and we are all wearing costumes and makeup. We will do the Red Riding Hood story. We will start it the right way, but, who knows how will we end it? Perhaps the big bad wolf will not get to eat her! And what if she eats the wolf?

It's a lot of fun to pretend to be someone else. Would you like to try it with your friends?

Let's set the scenery and invent

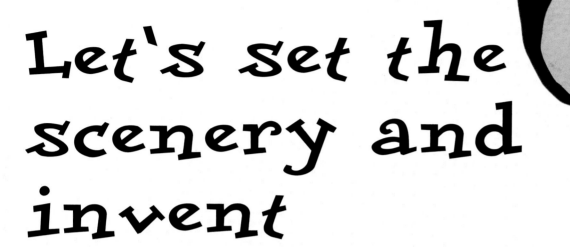

One thing is missing: The scenery for the story! We need a carriage, a house, and a basket with apples. We look around and find what we want: An upturned chair will be the carriage. We will build the house under the table and use some old bedcovers for walls, and the apples will come from the refrigerator. Now the show can start.

Shadow theater

Don't think all theaters are like this one, the actor tells us. There is street theater, without props or scenery; there is theater with puppets or marionettes, which are like puppets but hanging from strings. And in shadow theater, what people see are the shadows of actors and things behind a sheet.

Puppets

There are many kinds of puppets. We can make them by painting our fingers, or using a glove or a sock. Ann loves playing with puppets, even when she is by herself. When her friends come over, they play with different kinds of puppets: Some are painted on their own fingers, others are figures they cut from different materials and glue to a stick, and still others are lovely puppets they buy in stores.

Sometimes they also make masks with materials they find around the house or they even improvise a theater with some chairs and some cloth.

Harder still

"And finally, the circus! No, I didn't forget," the actor explains, "but the circus is not really a theater. Circus people don't make believe they are something different; they just perform very, very difficult tricks: They walk on a tightrope, or ride bicycles that only have one wheel, they jump in the air from one flying trapeze to another, or they juggle ten balls at a time as if it were the easiest thing in the world!"

Let's make a circus

With a little imagination you can play even if you don't have any toys. You can make believe you are walking on a tightrope just by following the slab lines on the pavement and hop!—a pretend triple somersault, just by jumping from one slab to the next. Wow! That was scary!

That is how one starts at the circus!

A VERY SIMPLE THEATER

Take a large empty carton and make a cut on each side and another on top, as shown in the drawing. On a piece of cardboard draw two characters for your theater play. Cut out the characters and stick a cardboard strip on the back with adhesive tape. On another piece of cardboard draw the background and attach a strip at the top. You can draw as many backgrounds and characters as you wish and continue changing them.

STICK PUPPETS

Draw on a carton a character you want to represent. Then cut out the character with scissors and attach a stick to the back of the figure using some adhesive tape. Lollipop sticks are excellent. You can make as many figures as you want. Trust me, you'll have great puppets to play with!

MITTEN PUPPETS

Take a mitten, some buttons, and old yarn. Put the mitten on your hand and imagine what kind of character you can make out of it. A monster that eats cookies? A gopher? Or maybe a mouse? Sew the buttons where the eyes go and use some yarn for the hair. Make a mustache with very thin black cardboard strips ... or some bristles from the broom.

If you use a long sock to make the puppet, you can make a snake or the neck of a giraffe. Take some socks and mittens, try them on, and see what they suggest to you.

LET'S MAKE THE DÉCOR

You can invent many interesting things for your décor: Tables, turned upside down, can be trains, ships, and airplanes; chairs can be cars or canoes; and a table covered with paper can be a cave or a tower.
If you find a huge box—the kind that holds TVs or refrigerators—you can create a house. Cut the box as shown to make doors and windows, and color it with crayons.

MIRRORING

This is a game to play in pairs. Stand in front of your friend and imitate (in silence) every thing he does—the faces he makes, his movements, his postures—as if you were a real mirror.
Have fun!

A Guide for parents

A Guide Guide

PLAYING

Invent characters, provide a lot of details about them, and make up a situation in which all the characters appear. Resort to past family conflicts, express feelings and sensations through mimicry, alter known tales, invent stories happening in the past or future. The game "Follow Me" may also be used: One child starts the story and then the next child continues it. Turns must be respected and time limits set.

NOISES, SOUNDS, AND WHISPERS

Have the children listen to the sounds of the city at night, and have them notice how the sounds change as night becomes day. Suggest the sounds of a stream or the noises of a mysterious castle. Sounds can be reproduced using the mouth, hands, or feet. You can make thousands of sound effects: With a jar full of beans, with wood and metal spoons, with pots and pans. It's fun for parents to think what materials can be used to reproduce certain sounds and suggest them to the children. And if the kids don't think they are a good idea, they may suggest different materials!

A TRUNK FULL OF SURPRISES

A great help in playing theater is having a trunk full of costumes: Fabrics, old garments, hats, ribbons, colorful handkerchiefs, wigs, whatever. It is much better if the costumes are not already made, in order to not limit the kind of character the children choose to be. Most of all, it is important that the children feel free when playing; they should not worry if the fabric they are wearing for a costume gets torn or dirty. It may be fun to visit friends and relatives to collect items for the trunk, as everybody has something that can be used. And let's not forget makeup!

BODY EXPRESSION

When we play theater with small children, we should forget the theater grownups play. For the kids, memorizing parts, portraying a character that is in no way related to them, or wearing costumes carefully so they will not be ruined is no fun at all and they may end up hating theater forever. But what about pretending they are a balloon being inflated and deflated, waves on a stormy day, or clouds that travel blown by the wind? We can ask the group to imitate the jungle: Different animals, rivers, plants, and birds. Each child chooses his or her role until they all agree.